WHEN IS TOMORROW?

BY *Nancy Dingman* WATSON

PICTURES BY *Aldren A. Watson*

NEW YORK   Alfred A. KNOPF

Library of Congress Catalog Card Number: 55-8939

© NANCY DINGMAN WATSON, 1955

THIS IS A BORZOI BOOK,
PUBLISHED BY ALFRED A. KNOPF, INC.

Distributed in Canada by Random House of Canada, Limited, Toronto.

To Bud

"Tomorrow we're going to Squirrel Island!" said Linda. "But Peter, when is tomorrow?"

"When you get out of bed, and we're on our way, that will be tomorrow," said Peter.

The next morning, Linda got out of bed and ate a good big breakfast of eggs she had gathered herself, and homemade bread and farm butter, honey and a tall glass of milk.

Peter and Mother packed the back of the car up to the roof, with just a little square place for Linda to curl up and take a nap if she wanted to. Then they all kissed Daddy good-by three times and started on their way.

"Now Peter," said Linda, as she settled herself beside her favorite rabbit doll. "Is this tomorrow?"

"No," said Peter. "This is today."

"When is tomorrow?" asked Linda.

They drove miles and miles from Vermont to New Hampshire, and from New Hampshire up the coast of Maine. Linda began to see drawbridges and sea gulls and sailing ships. At last they came to the harbor town where they would get a boat to the island. Mother drove the car out onto the wharf and parked.

Linda danced up and down. "Peter!" she said again. "Peter, when is tomorrow?"

Just then the *Nellie G.* blew her red-and-white-striped whistle and they all climbed aboard.

Past the breakwater they steamed, past the lighthouse and some fishing boats and a big oil tanker. In the distance the Christmas trees on the island lifted their heads out of the blue breakers.

"There's Squirrel Island," said Peter. "Tomorrow we'll go for a sail. Hop off, now!"

The next afternoon, Peter and Linda went for a sail around Squirrel Island. The salt water sprayed them and the sun dried them off. On the south side of the island it was rough and breezy and Linda pulled on Peter's sweater, but on the other side it was warm and calm and she pulled it off again.

"This is fine, Peter," said Linda. "Is this tomorrow?"

"No," said Peter, "this is today. Tomorrow we will go fishing in the cove."

The next day Peter made Linda a fishing line, and off they went to the cove. Peter caught three fish and gave one of them to Linda. It was warm in the sun, on the rocks of the cove.

"This is nice, Peter," said Linda. "Is this tomorrow?"

"No," said Peter, "this is today. But never mind. Tomorrow we'll go to the beach. We'll dig for clams when the tide is low. Tomorrow will be fun."

The next morning after breakfast, Peter and Linda went to the beach and dug clams. They picked up wavy pink shells and found sand dollars and crabs and starfish. The wet sand tickled Linda's bare toes and the clams squirted little fountains of water from their bubble holes.

"This is a nice tomorrow," said Linda.

Peter laughed. "This isn't tomorrow, this is today. But tomorrow we'll swim in the cove and play in the sand when the tide is high. We'll take a picnic," said Peter.

"Oh," said Linda. "I can hardly wait for tomorrow!"

The next day Peter and Linda took a picnic lunch to the beach, and built roads in the sand, and swam in the bay. When they got hungry, Linda gathered bits of silvery driftwood so Peter could build a fire.

They poked forks through their hot dogs and roasted them over the coals. They had carrot sticks and tomatoes and buttered buns and lots of cold milk. Then they had bananas and raisin cookies and more cold milk.

"This is a good picnic," said Linda. "I like tomorrow."

"This isn't tomorrow," said Peter. "This is today. Tomorrow Mr. Sweers will take us lobstering."

The next morning, Peter and Linda tiptoed through the house and out into the gray, rolling fog. The morning light was just creeping up from the sea when they boarded the lobster boat. Around the island they went in Mr. Sweers's boat, with the sea gulls swooping and calling around them in the shivery morning.

Each time they came to a bright red and white buoy, Mr. Sweers hauled up the heavy trap beneath. Inside were crabs and lobsters, prickly round sea urchins and live starfish.

"This is fun," said Linda. "Tomorrow is really nice. Is this tomorrow, Peter?"

"No," said Peter, "but tomorrow is our last day on Squirrel Island. Tomorrow we will pack our bags and get on the *Nellie G.* and say good-by to the island. Tomorrow we are going home."

The next day Linda and Peter helped Mother pack. Linda had three pails of pretty stones and shells and sea creatures to take home to Daddy. Peter had two big grain bags filled with red and white, green and blue and orange buoys. He also had a broken lobster trap he thought could be fixed.

The captain of the *Nellie G.* helped them onto the boat, and told them salty stories as they sailed over to the mainland.

Peter and Linda were sorry to leave Squirrel Island. "Good-by," they called to the captain.

But that night, when her own daddy came to tuck Linda into her own little bed at home, Linda said, "This is the best tomorrow of all!"